Malevolence and Mandrake

Drawing: Mauricet
Script: Virginie Vanholme
Colour work: Laurent Carpentier

Inking pages 1 to 18: Lee Oaks

9th CINEBOOK
The 9th Art Publisher

Original title: Mort de Trouille – Maléfice et Mandragore

Original edition: © Casterman, 2003
by Mauricet & Vanholme
www.casterman.com

English translation: © 2008 Cinebook Ltd

Translator: Luke Spear
Lettering and text layout: Imadjinn
Printed in Spain by Just Colour Graphic

This edition first published in Great Britain in 2009 by
CINEBOOK Ltd
56 Beech Avenue
Canterbury, Kent
CT4 7TA
www.cinebook.com

A CIP catalogue record for this book
is available from the British Library

ISBN 978-1-905460-77-9

CINEBOOK
The 9th Art Publisher

THAT'S ENOUGH, ASTAROTH! DON'T TOUCH HIM!

MEOOOW

EEEE!!

HSSS

SO, MY PRETTY... WERE WE TRYING TO ESCAPE?!

AH...

H-HELP! LET ME GO!

H-HELP ME!

YOU CAN SHOUT ALL YOU WANT HERE, BUT NOBODY WILL SAVE YOU.

MEANIE! YOU'RE SO MEAN!

COME ON, HURRY UP, SIT DOWN!

I HAVE SOME GOOD NEWS AND SOME BAD NEWS...

THE BAD NEWS IS ONE OF YOUR FELLOW PUPILS WON'T BE COMING TO CLASS TODAY. IN FACT, THOMAS DISAPPEARED TWO DAYS AGO, MUCH TO HIS PARENTS' CONCERN.

LET'S HOPE THAT HE'S JUST RUN AWAY. AND CAN YOU PLEASE CONTACT THE POLICE OR COME TO SEE ME AFTER SCHOOL IF YOU KNOW ANYTHING ABOUT THIS DISAPPEARANCE?

RIGHT... NOW LET'S MOVE ON TO THE BETTER NEWS. WE'RE GOING TO WELCOME A NEW STUDENT TO OUR CLASS...

EMMA?

THOMAS IS MISSING? IS THAT A JOKE?

YEAH, HE'S SUCH A TEACHER'S PET, IT'S NOT LIKE HIM TO MISS LESSONS.

2

COME IN, THEN, DON'T BE SHY.

CHILDREN, THIS IS EMMA CORPESCU.

ERR.. HI.

COULD YOU BRIEFLY INTRODUCE YOURSELF?...

HOT! WE'RE SO LUCKY.

MAX...

I'M EMMA AND I'M 14 YEARS OLD. I'M FROM ROMANIA, ALTHOUGH I'VE LIVED IN FRANCE, SPAIN... ALL OVER EUROPE, IN FACT. I FOLLOW MY... MY MOTHER AND HER WORK.

WHAT DO YOUR PARENTS DO?

MY FATHER IS DEAD. AND MY MOTHER IS... HOW DO YOU SAY? BIOCHEMIST. OR SOMETHING LIKE THAT. SHE'S A SCIENTIST.

DO YOU HAVE BROTHERS AND SISTERS?

I HAD A BIG SISTER, BUT SHE DIED... A LONG TIME AGO.

TALK ABOUT GOOD NEWS... IT'S LIKE STAND-UP COMEDY. I THINK WE'LL HAVE FUN WITH HER...

HEE HEE

3

THE WITCHES OF MARS! I HEARD THEY EXISTED, BUT I DIDN'T WANT TO BELIEVE IT.

OH, MASTER! WE ARE YOUR SERVANTS —YOUR WISH IS OUR COMMAND.

SILENCE! I THINK WE'RE BEING WATCHED!

UH OH!

TO BE CONTINUED

CRAP!

IT'S ALWAYS THE SAME! IN TWO PARTS...

22 TO BE CONTINUED

SAY, ROBIN. CAN YOU LEND ME THE NEXT ONE?

SURE.

CAN I SIT WITH YOU?

?!

AS THERE'S A SPARE SEAT, I THOUGHT...

NO!

4

WE'D RATHER IT WAS YOU, MAX...

HE IS TOO CUTE...

HEEHEE!

CAN'T YOU SEE WE'RE BUSY WITH GUY THINGS?!

WHY DON'T YOU GO AND SIT AT THE GIRLS' TABLE? OVER THERE!

DON'T LISTEN TO THEM, EMMA. THEY'RE A BIT LIMITED... YOU CAN SIT HERE IF YOU WANT.

WHAT ARE YOU EATING? IT LOOKS LIKE MARTIAN FOOD...

IT'S TRUE. IT HAS A STRANGE COLOUR.

IT'S SARMA. A ROMANIAN SPECIALITY. YOU WANT TO TRY SOME?

NO, THANKS... ERR... HAVE YOU MADE ANY GIRL FRIENDS YET?

NO... ANYWAY, I'VE ALWAYS PREFERRED TO PLAY WITH BOYS.

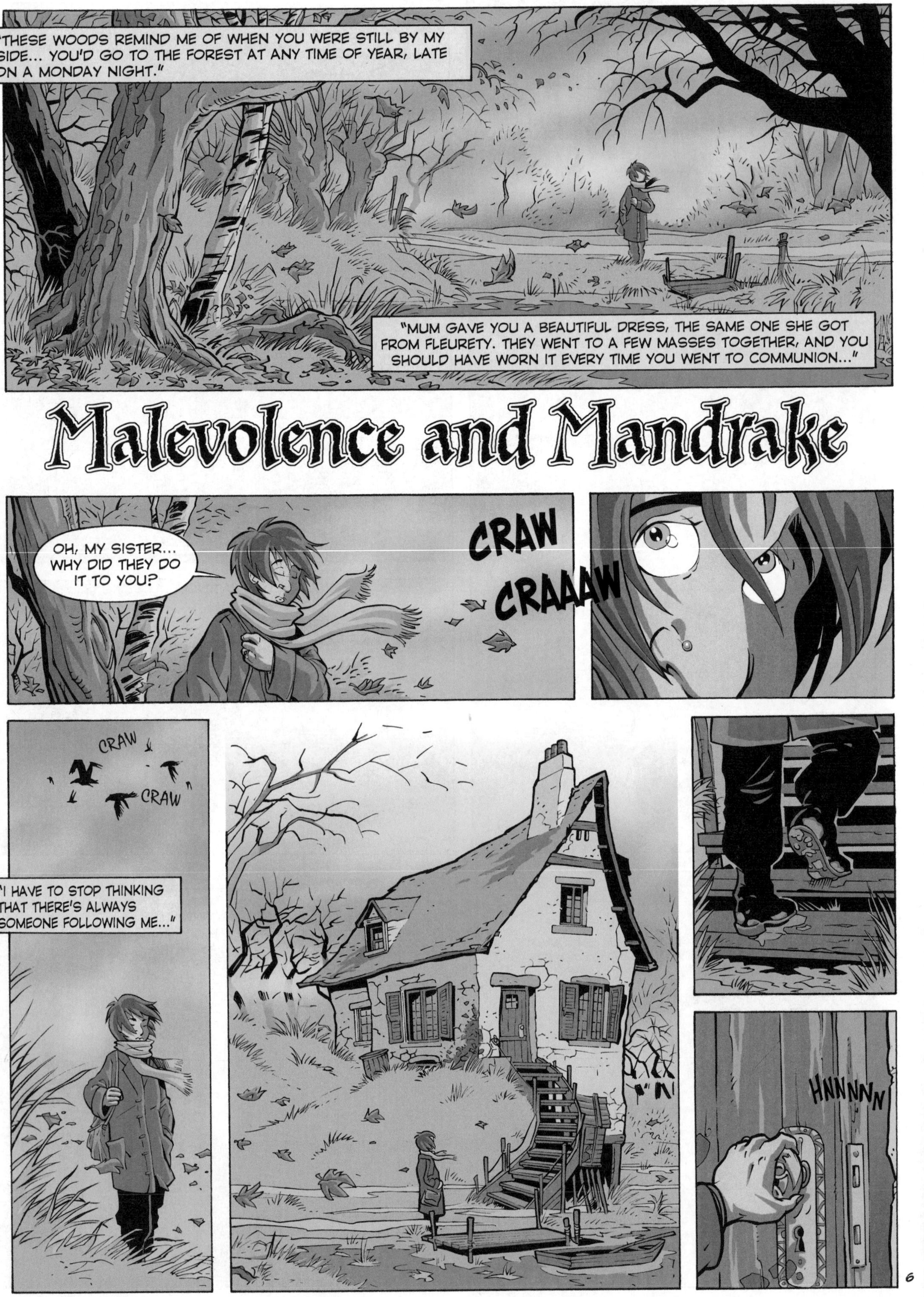
"THESE WOODS REMIND ME OF WHEN YOU WERE STILL BY MY SIDE... YOU'D GO TO THE FOREST AT ANY TIME OF YEAR, LATE ON A MONDAY NIGHT."
"MUM GAVE YOU A BEAUTIFUL DRESS, THE SAME ONE SHE GOT FROM FLEURETY. THEY WENT TO A FEW MASSES TOGETHER, AND YOU SHOULD HAVE WORN IT EVERY TIME YOU WENT TO COMMUNION..."
Malevolence and Mandrake
OH, MY SISTER... WHY DID THEY DO IT TO YOU?
CRAW
CRAAAW
CRAW
CRAW
"I HAVE TO STOP THINKING THAT THERE'S ALWAYS SOMEONE FOLLOWING ME..."
HNNNNN
6

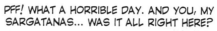

HELLO! I'M HOME...

CACRAAAW

PFF! WHAT A HORRIBLE DAY. AND YOU, MY SARGATANAS... WAS IT ALL RIGHT HERE?

CRAW

I'M HAPPY TO BE HOME AT LAST...

CROOAAW

7

9

DRILLING

COME ALONG, CALM DOWN! JUST LISTEN FOR TWO MORE MINUTES...

DON'T FORGET THE TEST ON CHAPTER 13, NEXT FRIDAY... AND TOMORROW, DO EXERCISES 12 TO 20, WITH...

WELL! DID YOU SEE THE SUBJECT?! THAT OLD BAT'S BLOWN A FUSE!

OH, IT'S NOT THAT HARD. YOU'RE EXAGGERATING...

THERE'RE ONLY FOUR FORMULAS TO LEARN BY HEART, AND THE REST IS JUST APPLICATION.

WELL, I DON'T FEEL VERY APPLIED WHEN IT COMES TO MATHS...

I'M SURE YOU'D BE MORE PASSIONATE IF YOU WERE BEING TESTED ON THE LATEST VIDEO GAMES.

YEAH! THAT'S REAL LIFE: GAMES, CRISPS AND COKE!

DON'T LOOK NOW, MAX... YOUR GIRLFRIEND'S FOLLOWING US.

WHAT ARE YOU ON ABOUT?!

IT'S THE END OF THE DAY. EMMA'S GOING HOME LIKE EVERYONE ELSE...

HMM... I DUNNO. I STILL THINK SHE'S A BIT STRANGE... DID YOU SEE WHAT SHE EATS?!

NO, I TASTED ONE OF HER GREEN SNACKS AT LUNCHTIME. IT WAS GREAT!...

ARE YOU TRYING TO GET YOURSELF KILLED?

8

SOPHIE?!... YOUR BROTHER'S HERE. GET YOUR BAG. YOU CAN GO.

HI, SCAMP. HOW ARE YOU?

HI, MAX! HI, BRO!

ROBIN, CAN YOU HELP ME CARRY MY THINGS?

IT WEIGHS A TONNE! WHAT HAVE YOU GOT IN IT?

WELL, MISS GAVE US A SPECIAL HALLOWEEN DAY...

SHE EXPLAINED WHERE IT CAME FROM. WE ALSO READ A LOAD OF STORIES ABOUT WITCHES. EVEN IN RUSSIA, THEY HAVE ONE CALLED BABA YAGA. SHE FLIES IN A CAULDRON...

AND SHE EATS LITTLE BOYS! IT'S GREAT, EH?!

SEE THAT? JUST LIKE IN JARVIS...

BAH...

ALL THAT STUFF'S RUBBISH! WITCHES DON'T EXIST.

BOOF

HOW CLUMSY! I'VE DROPPED ALL MY BOOKS.

WAIT, LEAVE IT... I'LL PICK THEM UP.

9

RIGHT, ARE YOU COMING NOW? MAX?... AREN'T WE GOING TO PLAY SOME JARVIS 2 ON MY CONSOLE AT HOME?...

ERR... GO ON, I'M COMING.

WELL, THERE YOU GO, IT'S ALL IN THERE. AT LEAST, I THINK. GOODBYE.

HUH? **WOW!** I DIDN'T ASK FOR THAT MUCH!

WELL, I DON'T GET IT.

YEAH, WHAT'S HE LIKE ABOUT THAT UGLY REDHEAD? WHAT'S SHE GOT OVER ME?

HEY, I'M HERE! WAIT FOR ME!

"WELL?... WHAT'S THE MATTER?"

"CAN'T YOU HELP SOMEONE WITHOUT GETTING SHOT?"

TAKE THAT, SCUM! AND THAT!

GO ON, MAX! BLOW THOSE MARS WITCHES AWAY!

GO LEFT, MATE! LOOK OUT!

OOPS! YEAH, YOU BLASTED HIM!

BLAM BLAM BLAM

END OF LEVEL 4
PLAYER 1   527
PLAYER 2   475

WELL PLAYED! YOU'VE NEVER BEEN THIS FAR IN THE GAME BEFORE! I WONDER WHAT'S NEXT...!

MATHS HOMEWORK. WE HAVE AN HOUR BEFORE MY PARENTS GET BACK...

ARE YOU KIDDING? YOU ONLY NEED 20 MINUTES TO SOLVE THOSE EQUATIONS...

THAT GIVES US PLENTY OF TIME FOR A LAST ROUND. ROBIN "THE CALCULATOR" AND MAX "THE DEVASTATOR" ARE GOING TO BLOW THAT SCORE AWAY!

SO, MY PRETTY?...

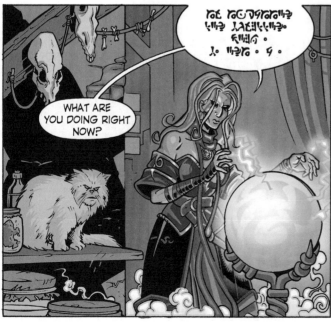

WHAT ARE YOU DOING RIGHT NOW?

EVEN IF YOU WERE ARMED, YOU COULDN'T DO ANYTHING TO ME, MAX...

HAHAHA

11

IN A FEW HOURS, YOU'LL BE COMPLETELY UNDER MY SPELL. IT WILL BE IMPOSSIBLE FOR YOU TO ESCAPE ME!

CRAAAW

CRAW

AH, THERE YOU ARE, SARGATANAS...

YOU STILL HAVEN'T FOUND THE PLACE, HAVE YOU?

CRAAA

DON'T GIVE UP. WE'LL FIND OUT JUST WHERE MY MANDRAKE LIES.

WE'LL SOON BE REUNITED.

I'VE JUST LAID MY HAND ON A SECOND VICTIM. NOW IT'S JUST A QUESTION OF TIME...

COME, LET'S RETURN TO THE FOREST...

12

CRAAAW

I KNOW YOU'RE HERE SOMEWHERE...

WE'RE IN THE RIGHT FOREST, BUT IT WAS SO LONG AGO...

I'VE FORGOTTEN.

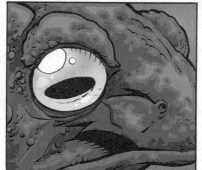

I'LL FIND YOU. I HAVE TO!... WE ONLY HAVE TWO NIGHTS LEFT TO CARRY OUT THE FINAL SACRIFICE.

13

YOU KNOW, THIS IS THE FIRST TIME I'VE BEEN CALLED TO THE HEADMASTER'S OFFICE...

I'VE GOT A SEASON TICKET. DON'T WORRY... YOU GET USED TO IT.

HEADMASTER

NEXT!

THIS IS MAX MORNET. HE'S IN THOMAS'S CLASS TOO.

TAKE A SEAT HERE, IN FRONT OF ME.

AS YOU MAY SUSPECT, WE'RE HERE TO INVESTIGATE THOMAS'S DISAPPEARANCE. I'D LIKE YOU TO ANSWER A FEW QUESTIONS...

CAN YOU TELL ME IF YOUR CLASSMATE'S BEHAVIOUR HAS SEEMED NORMAL RECENTLY?

ERM... YES. HE SEEMED TO BE HIMSELF.

DID HE TALK TO YOU ABOUT ANY FAMILY PROBLEMS?

NO, BUT HE'S REALLY NOT A FRIEND, YOU KNOW...

YOU THINK HE COULD HAVE RUN AWAY?

PFF... I WOULDN'T SAY THAT'S HIS STYLE.

AND IN THE AREA, YOU HAVEN'T NOTICED ANYTHING UNUSUAL? PEOPLE ACTING STRANGELY, STRANGERS ROAMING ABOUT THE SCHOOL?

NO, SIR... NOTHING AT ALL.

14

"YOU CAN GO, MAX."

YOU'RE UP, MATE! I'LL WAIT HERE, OK?

WELL, THAT WAS WEIRD.

MAX...

?

EMMA!? I DIDN'T HEAR YOU COMING...

I CAN BE VERY DISCREET WHEN I NEED TO BE.

LOOK! I'VE GOT SOMETHING FOR YOU...

EH?!

NOW, YOU WILL OBEY ME... COME!

YES.

AND CARRY MY BAG BACK TO MY PLACE!

YES.

WHY'S HE STILL HANGING AROUND WITH THAT GINGER?

HE'S SUPPOSED TO COME HOME WITH US... THIS ISN'T RIGHT. I'M FOLLOWING THEM.

15

NOW, JUST WHERE ARE THEY GOING...

WHAT IS THAT THING?

EEK...

TCHING

TCHINGELING

MAX?!

PULL YOURSELF TOGETHER.

SO THIS IS WHERE EMMA LIVES?!

IT'S STRANGE. DAD AND I HAVE WALKED AROUND HERE LOADS OF TIMES... BUT I'VE NEVER NOTICED THIS HOUSE!

16

COME ON, SOPHIE, BE BRAVE! GO AND TAKE A LOOK. MAX COULD BE IN DANGER...

OH, NO!

SHE... SHE WANTS TO BURY HIM?!

HAHAHA

HUH?!

AH! YOU'RE BACK WITH US!

WHERE AM I? WHAT ARE WE BOTH DOING HERE?

17

THINK BACK. YOU DIDN'T NOTICE ANYTHING AT ALL?...

WELL, NO... I CAN'T THINK OF A SINGLE THING. NOTHING OUT OF THE ORDINARY.

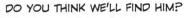

DO YOU THINK WE'LL FIND HIM?

I THINK THOMAS HAS JUST RUN AWAY... NOTHING TO WORRY ABOUT. BUT WE HAVE TO CONSIDER ALL EVENTUALITIES.

CAN I GO, SIR? MY LITTLE SISTER AND MY FRIEND ARE WAITING FOR ME... AND MY MOTHER WILL BE WORRIED IF WE GET HOME LATE.

RIGHT, NOW THAT YOU'VE HAD A GOOD LAUGH AND I'VE HAD A GOOD FRIGHT, COULD YOU CONSIDER UNTYING ME?

TSK TSK

I'VE GOT IT! YOU'VE GOT THE HOTS FOR ME AND YOU WON'T LET ME GO UNTIL AFTER YOU'VE ABUSED MY BODY...

COME ON, THEN! PUCKER UP!

YOU REALLY THINK THAT I FANCY YOU?...

MY POOR LITTLE MAX. HOW PRESUMPTUOUS YOU ARE!

WHEN YOU FIND OUT WHO I AM AND WHY I BROUGHT YOU HERE, YOU'LL BE LESS COCKY!

THIS CHICK HAS COMPLETELY LOST IT!

HAHAHAHAHA

18

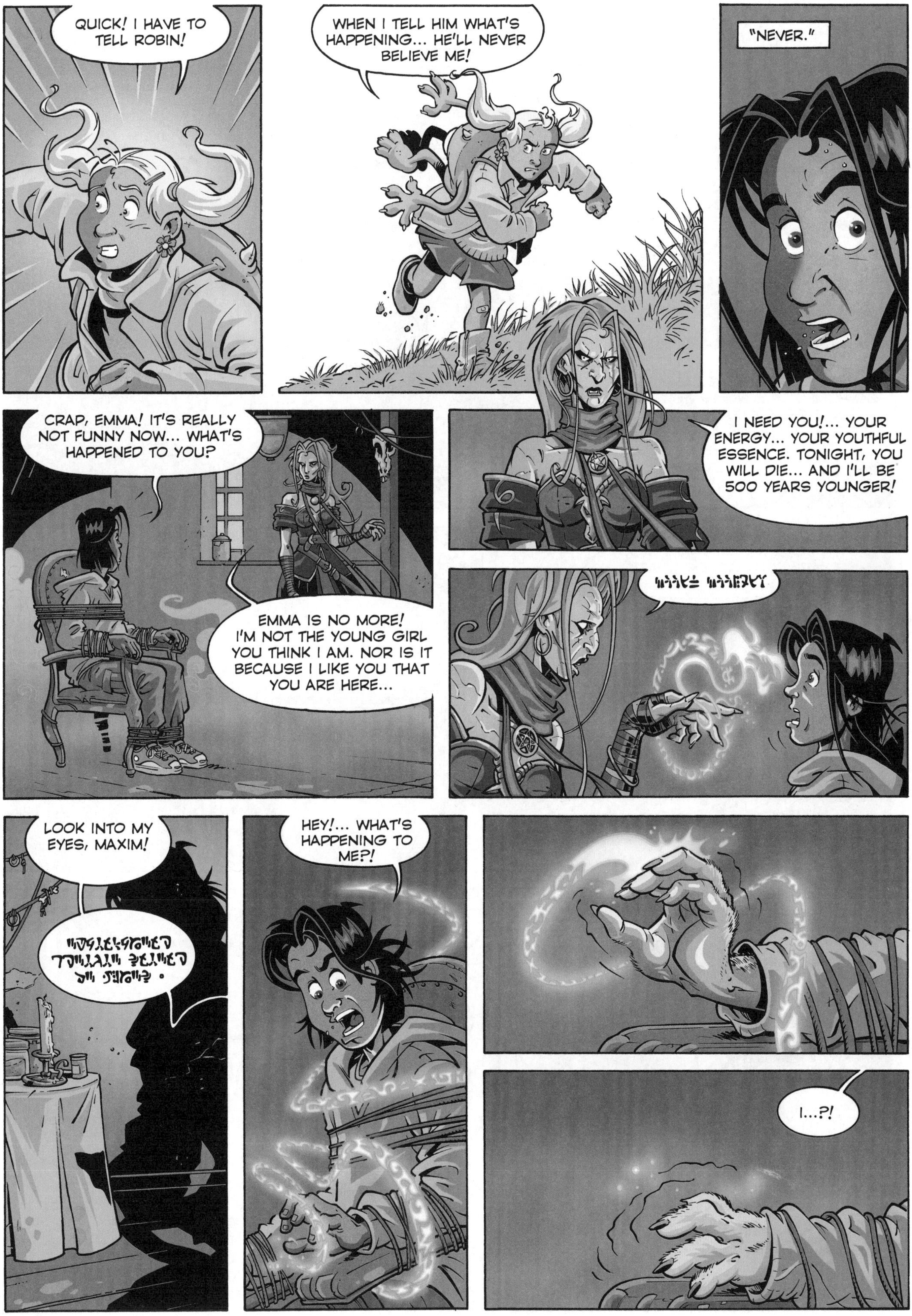
QUICK! I HAVE TO TELL ROBIN!
WHEN I TELL HIM WHAT'S HAPPENING... HE'LL NEVER BELIEVE ME!
"NEVER."
CRAP, EMMA! IT'S REALLY NOT FUNNY NOW... WHAT'S HAPPENED TO YOU?
EMMA IS NO MORE! I'M NOT THE YOUNG GIRL YOU THINK I AM. NOR IS IT BECAUSE I LIKE YOU THAT YOU ARE HERE...
I NEED YOU!... YOUR ENERGY... YOUR YOUTHFUL ESSENCE. TONIGHT, YOU WILL DIE... AND I'LL BE 500 YEARS YOUNGER!
LOOK INTO MY EYES, MAXIM!
HEY!... WHAT'S HAPPENING TO ME?!
I...?!

19

I'VE BEEN WAITING FOR 10 MINUTES NOW.

PUFF...

WELL, WHERE WERE YOU, FOR CRYING OUT LOUD?! YOU KNOW THAT YOU CAN'T LEAVE THE SCHOOL ALONE!

PUFF... PUFF!

SINCE THOMAS DISAPPEARED, YOU HAVE TO WAIT FOR ME. ON MUM'S ORDERS. WHEN SHE FINDS OUT... *GRR!* COME ON, LET'S GO HOME...

LISTEN TO ME! WE CAN'T GO HOME NOW... WE HAVE TO GO INTO THE FOREST. MAX IS IN TROUBLE!

WHAT!? YOU WENT WALKING IN THE DEAD WATER SWAMP WOODS? ARE YOU MAD, OR WHAT?...

ANYWAY, ANY MORE DELAYS ARE OUT OF THE QUESTION. WE'RE ALREADY LATE ENOUGH. I DON'T WANT TO BE TOLD OFF BECAUSE OF YOU!

ROBIN, I SWEAR IT'S SERIOUS! EMMA'S GONE MAD... SHE'S KIDNAPPED MAX, AND STRAPPED HIM TO A CHAIR!

?

THEN, SHE STARTED HITTING HIM!... AND HER HAIR STARTED TO GROW.

WHERE DO YOU GET THIS RUBBISH FROM?...

I'D BE VERY SURPRISED IF MAX LET HIMSELF GET BEATEN UP BY A GIRL...

YOU HAVE TO BELIEVE ME, BRO.

46

8434

VROOOM

I DEFINITELY BELIEVE THAT YOU'RE JEALOUS...

VROOM

20

22

"IN THE SABBAT RITUAL, WIZARDS AND WITCHES GATHER AROUND THE DEVIL. THEY OFFER HIM CHILDREN, WHO ARE THEN SACRIFICED AND EATEN DURING AN EXTRAVAGANT FEAST..."

IT LOOKS LIKE WITCHES PREFER TO EAT BOYS MORE THAN GIRLS...

"IF THESE BELIEFS MAKE EVEN THE MOST INCREDULOUS AMONGST US SMILE TODAY, REMAIN WARY OF INCANTATIONS, SPELLS AND OTHER MAGICAL RITES. THE DEVIL'S CREATURES CAN CHARM WITHOUT THEIR VICTIMS KNOWING IT..."

LOOK, IT EXPLAINS HOW TO PROTECT AGAINST THEM... "DRAW A CIRCLE OF SALT AROUND YOU. IT WILL STOP ANY EVIL FROM REACHING YOU."

"REFUSE TO SHAKE AN OUTSTRETCHED HAND. IT COULD...

PEEKABOO!

AAAH

IDIOT!

WHAT ARE YOU DOING IN MY ROOM? YOU KNOW I DON'T WANT YOU USING MY COMPUTER.

I'M DOING SOME INTERNET RESEARCH...

PFF... STILL INTO YOUR STUPID WITCH STORIES?

EEEEEEEE

!

21

WAS IT YOU SHOUTING, MUM? WHAT'S GOING ON?!

YOUR MOTHER SAW A LITTLE MOUSE, CHILDREN...

LITTLE?! THAT DIRTY BEAST WAS AS BIG AS A BEAVER!

WHILE YOU'RE AT IT... WHY NOT AN ELEPHANT?

RELAX! WE'LL CATCH IT...

AND THEN WE'LL THROW IT OUT.

THE MAIN THING IS MANAGING TO GET A HAND ON IT...

?!

THERE!

IT'S GOING UPSTAIRS!

GO ON, GIRL! CATCH IT! HISS HISS!

MRIAOW!

AYAAAAH!

TRY NOT TO HURT IT... IT MUST BE TERRIFIED.

CHECK MY ROOM, SOPHIE! I'LL TAKE THE BATHROOM.

OK!

COME ON, GIRL, FETCH! I'M COUNTING ON YOU...

MEOW

HAVE YOU GOT SOMETHING?! IS IT HIDING UNDER THE BED?...

DARN! I SHOULD HAVE TAKEN THE BROOM.

THIS DUMB TOY WILL DO IT.

JARVIS

THERE IT IS!

THIS TIME, YOU'RE DONE FOR.

?

NO! NOT WITH THAT JARVIS STATUE! IT'S COLLECTABLE!

YOU CAN TALK?! AND YOU'VE GOT... MAX'S VOICE?!

WELL, YES, BRAINBOX! IT'S ME!

GET BACK, KITTY. LEAVE HIM ALONE.

GEEZ LOUISE, THAT WAS CLOSE! I THOUGHT I'D HAD IT.

23

ROBIN, C'MERE! YOU HAVE TO SEE THIS.

WHAT? DID YOU CATCH IT?! THAT'S INCREDIBLE.

WAIT. THAT'S NOT THE ONLY SURPRISE.

ARE YOU SITTING DOWN?

"MEET MAX, THE MOUSE."

HI, BUDDY.

HUH?!

IS THIS A JOKE? A TRICK?!...

I WISH IT WAS. THAT'D SAVE ME FROM BEING COVERED IN FLEAS...

?!

HUP!

BUT, NO, IT'S ME... THAT WITCH TURNED ME INTO A MOUSE...

IT'S ALL EMMA'S FAULT.

YOU SEE? I WAS RIGHT.

WHAT'S THIS ALL ABOUT?

EMMA ISN'T THE NICE GIRL THAT EVERYONE THINKS SHE IS.

SHE'S AN OLD WITCH! SHE TAKES ON A STUDENT'S APPEARANCE TO APPROACH US WITHOUT AROUSING SUSPICION...

"SHE IS ONLY INTERESTED IN BOYS. SHE NEEDS THEM TO SURVIVE..."

"IF I UNDERSTAND IT RIGHT, SHE STEALS THE ENERGY FROM THEIR YOUTHFULNESS TO REGENERATE HERSELF. SHE TRANSFORMED ME INTO A MOUSE TO KEEP ME CAPTIVE UNTIL IT WAS TIME FOR THE RITUAL..."

24

"I WAS GOING TO BE PART OF THE SACRIFICE THAT'S TAKING PLACE TONIGHT, ON THE DAY OF THE DEAD..."

YOU HAVE TO TAKE ME BACK... THERE'S STILL A KID TO SAVE!

WHAT?

YES, I WASN'T ALONE. THOMAS HAS ALSO BEEN CAPTURED AND TRANSFORMED...

"EXCEPT HIS MOTHER DIDN'T GIVE HIM ENOUGH FLUORIDE WHEN HE WAS LITTLE. I COULD NEVER THANK MINE ENOUGH, AS I MANAGED TO CHEW THROUGH THE BARS OF MY CAGE IN NO TIME!"

UNFORTUNATELY, I DIDN'T HAVE TIME TO FREE THOMAS. SO, I PREFERRED TO ESCAPE ALONE AND WARN YOU GUYS.

WE HAVE TO HURRY. I SAW THAT SHE DUG A HOLE BIG ENOUGH FOR A CORPSE.

WE HAVE TO HELP THOMAS!

AND ME TOO, GUYS! I DON'T WANT TO BE A HAIRY MOUSE FOR THE REST OF MY DAYS!

I THINK YOU'RE CUTE LIKE THAT!

DON'T TOUCH ME OR I'LL BITE YOU!

HEEHEEHEE! COME ON, SOPHIE. WE'LL DEAL WITH MUM AND DAD.

THAT'S IT. WE GOT IT.

ROBIN THREW IT OUT...

VERY GOOD, CHILDREN.

MUM... IS MY COSTUME READY?

IT'S STILL TOO EARLY TO GO OUT AND CELEBRATE HALLOWEEN...

NO, IT ISN'T! THE LONGER WE WAIT, THE FEWER SWEETS THEY'LL HAVE!

25

SO, DON'T FORGET! YOU CAN BRING BACK PLENTY OF SWEETS, BUT YOU HAVE TO STAY WITH YOUR BROTHER.

YEAH! SWEETS OR I'LL CAST MY SPELLS!

SON, I'M COUNTING ON YOU. YOU LOOK AFTER HER...

"HAPPY HALLOWEEN, MY LOVES!"

"HAVE FUN, KIDS. AND COME BACK ON TIME... OR ELSE YOUR MOTHER WILL WAKE UP THE WHOLE NEIGHBOURHOOD..."

IT'S OKAY! I THINK WE'RE FAR ENOUGH AWAY NOW...

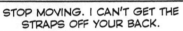

STOP MOVING. I CAN'T GET THE STRAPS OFF YOUR BACK.

GET ME OUT OF HERE! I CAN'T BREATHE!

WHAT THE?!...

GET THIS BOWTIE OFF ME OR THERE'LL BE TROUBLE!

HEEHEEHEE!

WHAT ARE YOU DOING IN THAT STUPID COSTUME?

WHY DON'T YOU ASK YOUR SISTER!

SOPHIE?...

WHAT? IT'S HALLOWEEN. HE NEEDS A COSTUME.

WE WEREN'T GOING TO WALK AROUND WITH HIM ALL NAKED IN THE STREET, WERE WE?... AND, I THINK IT SUITS HIM, THAT BARBIE JUMPER. HIS STOMACH'S JUST A LITTLE TOO BIG.

TOO BIG?! WAIT TILL I'M BACK TO MY NORMAL SIZE. YOU'LL BE SORRY.

SHHH, YOU TWO! SOMEONE'LL NOTICE US...

WELL, I DEFINITELY WON'T GO UNNOTICED WITH MY BALLERINA COSTUME.

HEY! LOOK!

26

IT'S MY SCHOOL FRIENDS! GIVE ME TWO MINUTES, BOYS. I'M JUST GOING TO SAY HELLO.

HI, SOPHIE! I LOVE YOUR COSTUME!

BUT...

YOURS, TOO. YOU BOTH LOOK GREAT! HAVE YOU ALREADY GOT LOTS OF SWEETIES?

WELL, WE'VE NEARLY FINISHED GOING AROUND... AND YOU?

WE'RE JUST STARTING.

WHAT ABOUT MAX? ISN'T HE WITH YOU? ...

SHE'S PUSHING IT A LITTLE TOO FAR NOW.

BLAHBLAH BLAH...

I KNEW IT. WE SHOULDN'T HAVE TAKEN HER WITH US.

THAT DUMB KID IS GOING TO GET IN OUR WAY. WE REALLY DIDN'T NEED HER...

OK, AND HOW WILL I EXPLAIN THAT TO MY PARENTS?

GO AND GET HER! YOU'RE OLDER THAN HER... SHE HAS TO DO AS YOU SAY, RIGHT?

SOPHIE, SAY GOODBYE TO YOUR FRIENDS. WE HAVE TO GO!

HURRY UP. WE DON'T HAVE ALL NIGHT!

WAIT, THERE'S MAUREEN. AND CHLOE, TOO...

GRRR. YOU'RE NO FUN!

DON'T FORGET THAT WE HAVE A VERY IMPORTANT MISSION.

HAVE YOU THOUGHT ABOUT A PLAN OF ATTACK?

DOES ANYONE WANT A MARS BAR?

YUM

27

29

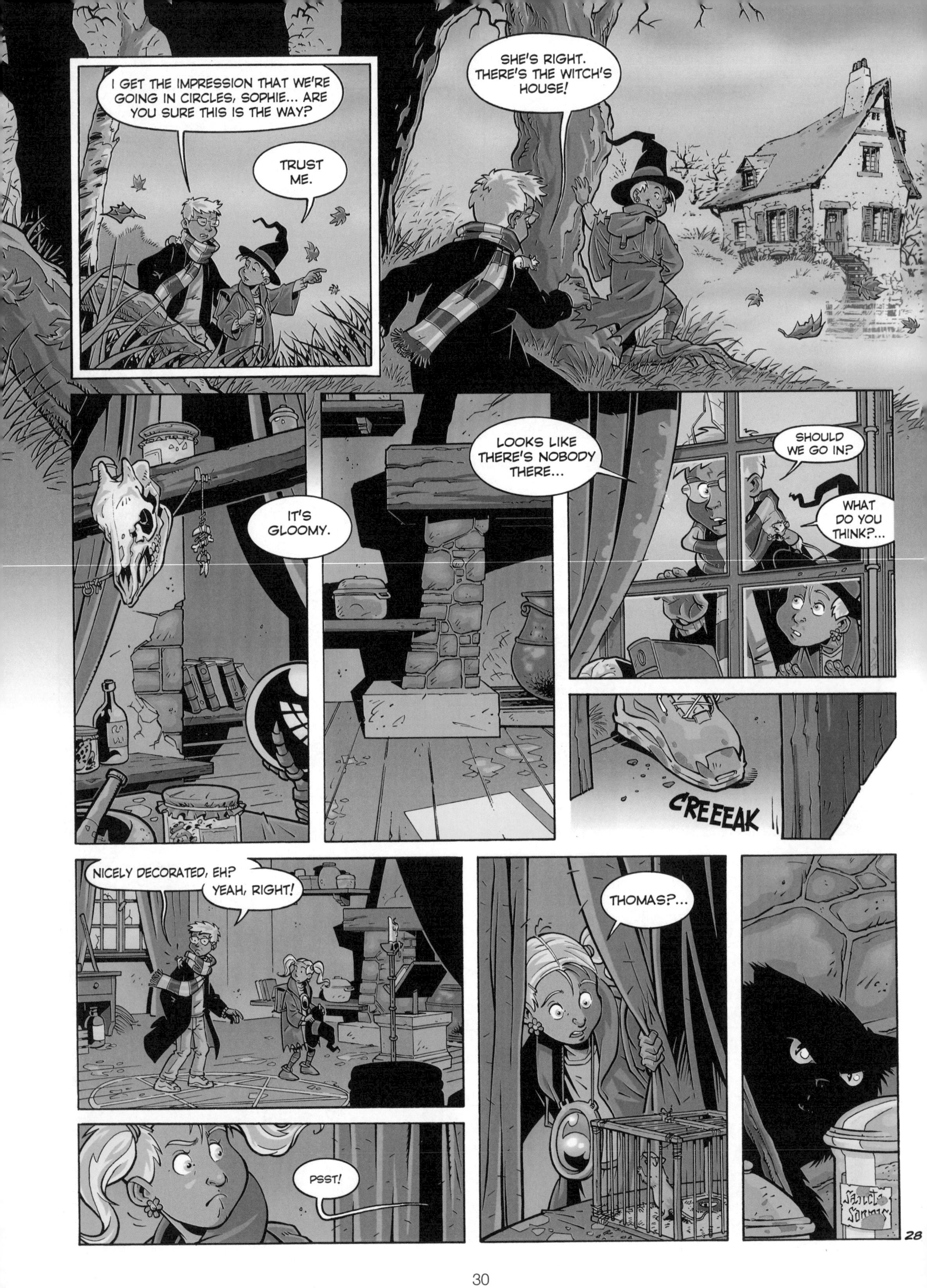
I GET THE IMPRESSION THAT WE'RE GOING IN CIRCLES, SOPHIE... ARE YOU SURE THIS IS THE WAY?
TRUST ME.
SHE'S RIGHT. THERE'S THE WITCH'S HOUSE!
IT'S GLOOMY.
LOOKS LIKE THERE'S NOBODY THERE...
SHOULD WE GO IN?
WHAT DO YOU THINK?...
CREEEAK
NICELY DECORATED, EH?
YEAH, RIGHT!
PSST!
THOMAS?...
28

I'M ROBIN'S SISTER. WE CAME TO SAVE YOU.

REALLY?! I WAS... I WAS SO SCARED. AND MAX? IS HE...

HE'S OKAY. YOU HAVE NOTHING TO FEAR. COME HERE.

MEOOOW

EEEEK! IT'S ASTAROTH!

HISSSS

CRIKEY! WHAT'S ALL THAT NOISE, SOPHIE?! DID YOU FIND THOMAS?

YES! I THINK THAT BLASTED CAT WANTS TO EAT HIM.

SQUEAK!

BANG

BOOM

BODOOM

MIAOOOW

IT'S AWFUL! THEY'VE DISAPPEARED INTO THE BUSHES. YOU THINK THAT NASTY THING WILL E... EAT HIM?

I'M WORRIED HE MIGHT...

THERE'S NOTHING WE CAN DO.

WHAT DO YOU MEAN, "NOTHING WE CAN DO"?! I CAN'T BELIEVE MY EARS! WHAT ABOUT ME? I'M NOT COUNTING ON BEING A RODENT ALL MY LIFE!

SNIFF... YOU'RE RIGHT, MAX, WE'RE SORRY.

I SUPPOSE THAT, LIKE ALL WITCHES, EMMA MUST HAVE A BOOK OF MAGIC SPELLS... WE COULD ALWAYS START BY FINDING THAT.

IF YOU'RE TALKING ABOUT A DUSTY OLD BOOK, WE DON'T STAND A CHANCE. THERE ARE HUNDREDS IN THIS PLACE!

29

SHTOK

COULD IT FINALLY BE?!...

SHTOK
SHTOK

MY MANDRAKE... YES... YES!

I'VE FOUND HER!

I'VE FOUND HER!

HAHAHAHAHA

30

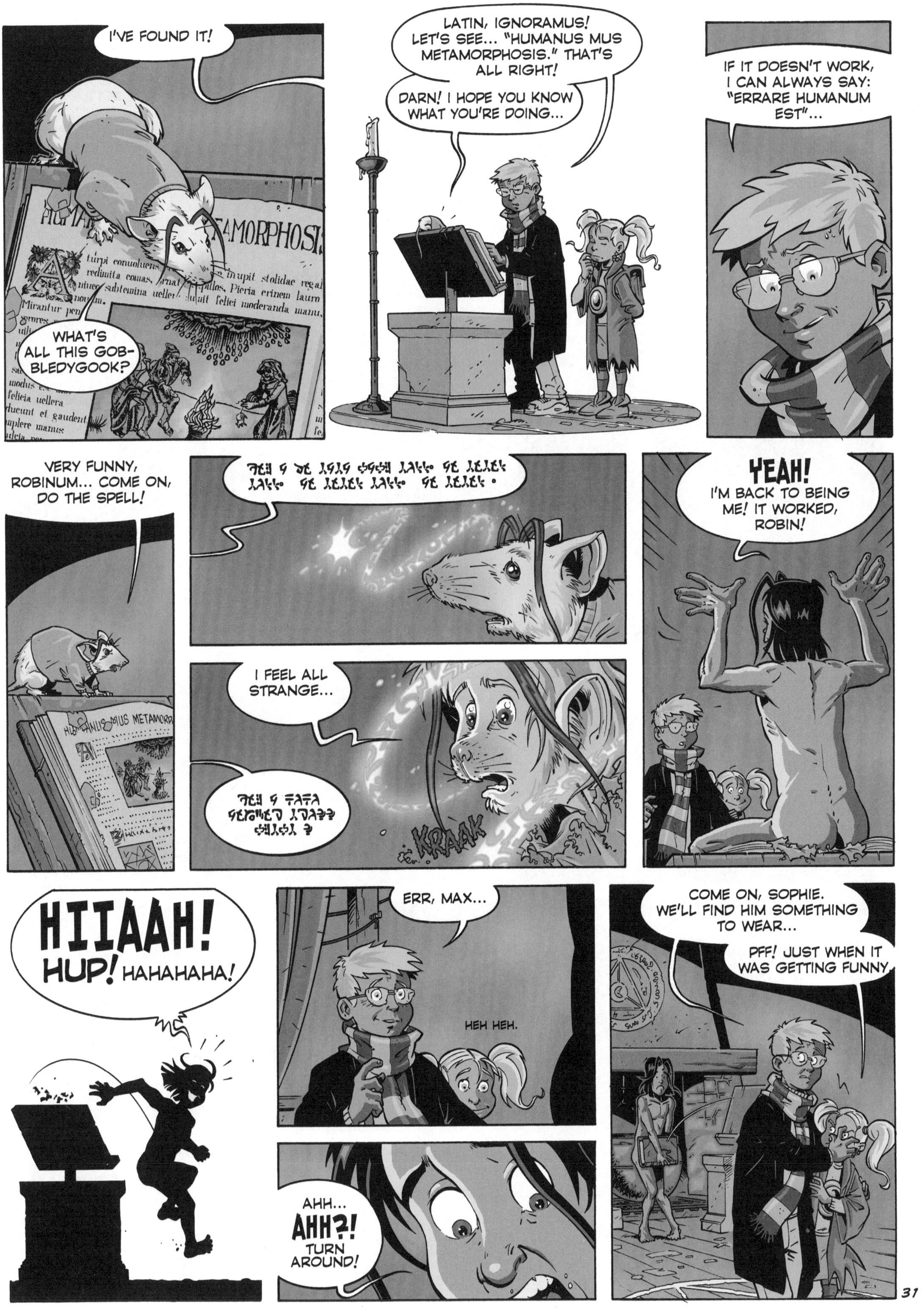
I'VE FOUND IT!
WHAT'S ALL THIS GOB-BLEDYGOOK?
LATIN, IGNORAMUS! LET'S SEE... "HUMANUS MUS METAMORPHOSIS." THAT'S ALL RIGHT!
DARN! I HOPE YOU KNOW WHAT YOU'RE DOING...
IF IT DOESN'T WORK, I CAN ALWAYS SAY: "ERRARE HUMANUM EST"...
VERY FUNNY, ROBINUM... COME ON, DO THE SPELL!
I FEEL ALL STRANGE...
KRAAK
YEAH! I'M BACK TO BEING ME! IT WORKED, ROBIN!
HIIAAH! HUP! HAHAHAHA!
ERR, MAX...
HEH HEH.
AHH... AHH?! TURN AROUND!
COME ON, SOPHIE. WE'LL FIND HIM SOMETHING TO WEAR...
PFF! JUST WHEN IT WAS GETTING FUNNY.
31

I PROMISE YOU WE LOOKED EVERYWHERE, MATE... BUT WE COULDN'T FIND YOUR CLOTHES.

GREAT! NOW I INHERIT POOR THOMAS'S AWFUL CLOTHES!

IT'S STILL BETTER THAN THE LITTLE PINK BARBIE JUMPER, ISN'T IT?

PFFF !

COME ON, SUPERMODEL. QUIT COMPLAINING. WE HAVE A SCORE TO SETTLE WITH A WITCH...

?

KIKI COOL

YOU'RE GOING TO GET IT, MALE-VOLENCE!

HOW WILL WE FIND HER?

GOOD QUESTION...

HEY, ROBIN... DID YOU HEAR WHAT SOPHIE JUST SAID?

WE DON'T HAVE THE SLIGHTEST IDEA...

?!

EEK!

HAHAHA

32

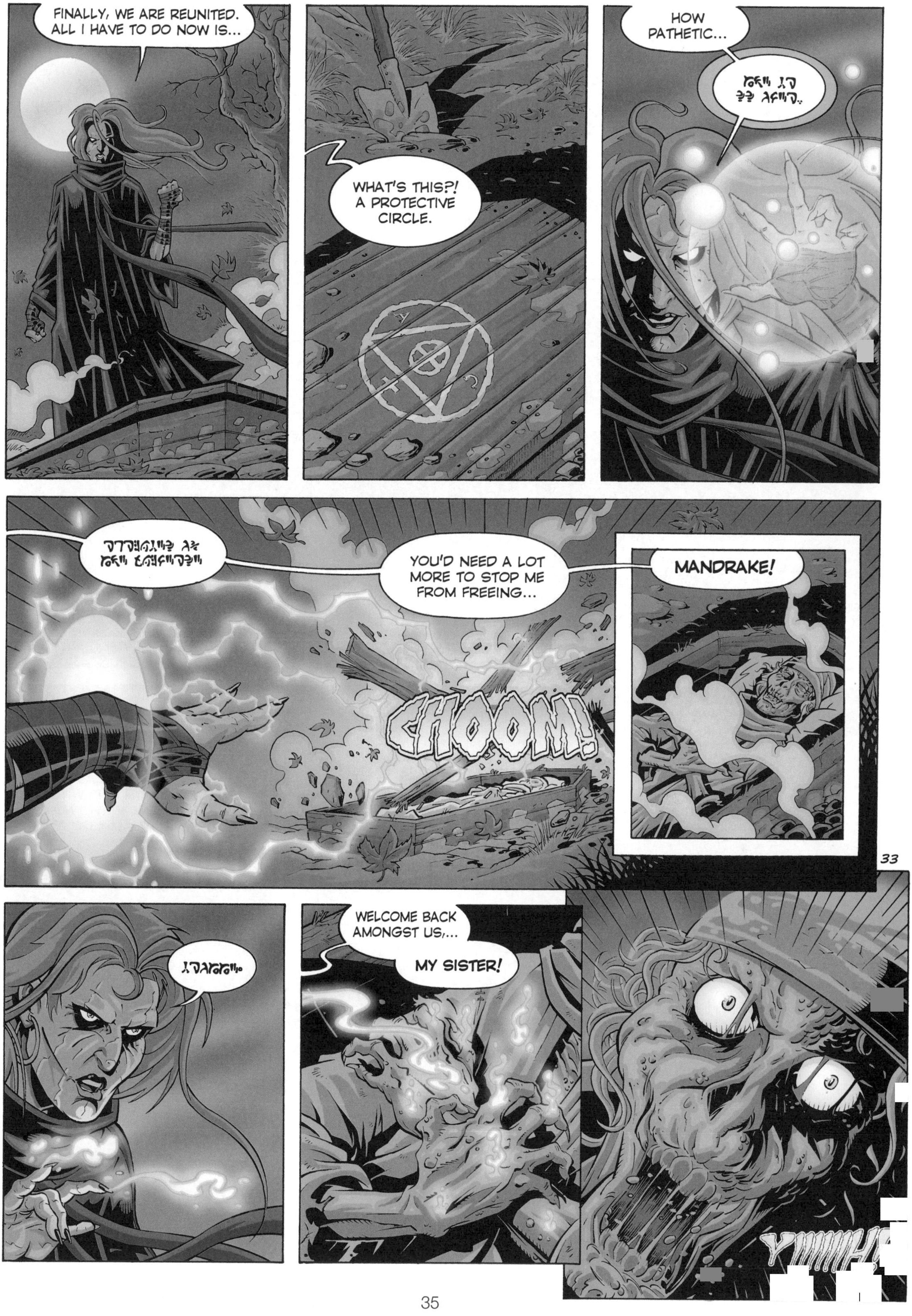
FINALLY, WE ARE REUNITED. ALL I HAVE TO DO NOW IS...
WHAT'S THIS?! A PROTECTIVE CIRCLE.
HOW PATHETIC...
YOU'D NEED A LOT MORE TO STOP ME FROM FREEING...
MANDRAKE!
CHOOM!
33
WELCOME BACK AMONGST US,...
MY SISTER!

MALEVOLENCE! FINALLY, YOU'VE FOUND ME...

IF ONLY YOU KNEW... I'VE BEEN WAITING FOR THIS MOMENT FOR TWO CENTURIES.

SISTER...

DO YOU THINK WE'LL STILL HAVE TIME TO REGENERATE OURSELVES?... WHERE IS THE ALIGNMENT?

"EVERYTHING IS PERFECT! WE COULDN'T HOPE FOR BETTER..."

"LOOK. THE EARTH TRACES A STRAIGHT LINE TO MARS AND JUPITER, PASSING BY THE MOON."

"AND THE COMET?"

IT WILL PASS IN UNDER AN HOUR... SO WE CAN PROCEED WITH THE RITUAL.

I HAD TO WAIT A LONG TIME... BUT I SEE THAT YOU HAVE BROUGHT TOGETHER THE PERFECT CONDITIONS.

IT WAS ALREADY TOUGH WITH ONE WITCH. BUT NOW, WITH TWO, WE'RE REALLY DONE FOR...

34

HAVE YOU GATHERED THE INGREDIENTS? YOU KNOW WHAT I'M TALKING ABOUT...

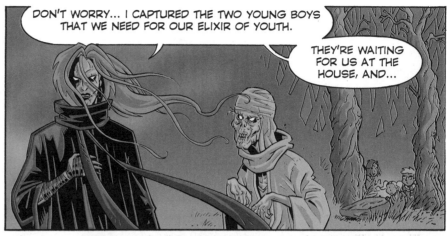

DON'T WORRY... I CAPTURED THE TWO YOUNG BOYS THAT WE NEED FOR OUR ELIXIR OF YOUTH.

THEY'RE WAITING FOR US AT THE HOUSE, AND...

SHH! ARE YOU SURE?

LOOKS LIKE THEY'VE SAVED US THE WALK. YOU'VE LOST YOUR SENSE OF SMELL, SISTER...

INDEED...

NOOO!

WHAK

UNGH!

SHHH

AAHHHHHH!

WELL, WELL... YOUNG ROBIN! YOU FOLLOWED YOUR FRIEND MAX OUT HERE... HOW KIND OF YOU.

LEAVE MY BROTHER ALONE!

YOU WILL JOIN US FOR THE SACRIFICE.

WELL, THIS IS A REAL FAMILY REUNION.

BE CAREFUL... SHE LOOKS LIKE A LITTLE WITCH.

A YOUNG SORCERESS, INDEED. LOOK AT THIS AMULET...

SNAP

I'M CERTAIN IT'S MAGIC AND BY RUBBING IT, WE CAN SUMMON A GENIE...

HAHA
HYIIIIHAHAHAH

THAT'S RIGHT! LAUGH IT UP! YOU'LL SEE, IN A FEW MINUTES...

YOU'LL BE LAUGHING A LOT LESS...

SALT

36

WITH THIS, YOU CAN'T GET NEAR ME!

A CIRCLE OF SALT!

YEAH! I FOUND THIS TRICK IN MY HALLOWEEN BOOK...

AND THERE'S EVEN A MAGIC SPELL THAT GETS RID OF WITCHES...

NASTY LITTLE PEST! IF YOU THINK YOU CAN DEFEAT MALEVOLENCE... TAKE THAT!

WHAK

WOW!

NOT BAD! BUT YOUR SPELL DOESN'T WORK... TRALALA!

YOU WILL DIE!

SISTER! WE'RE RUNNING OUT OF TIME! FORGET THE GIRL...

LET'S TAKE CARE OF THE BOY. THE TIME IS NEAR, AND WE STILL HAVE TO GO BACK TO THE HOUSE.

37

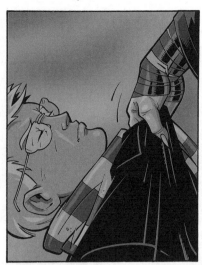

LET'S HURRY. I'M FEELING WEAK...

PSST... WITCHY!

...

ZING

GAME OVER.

POK   38

40

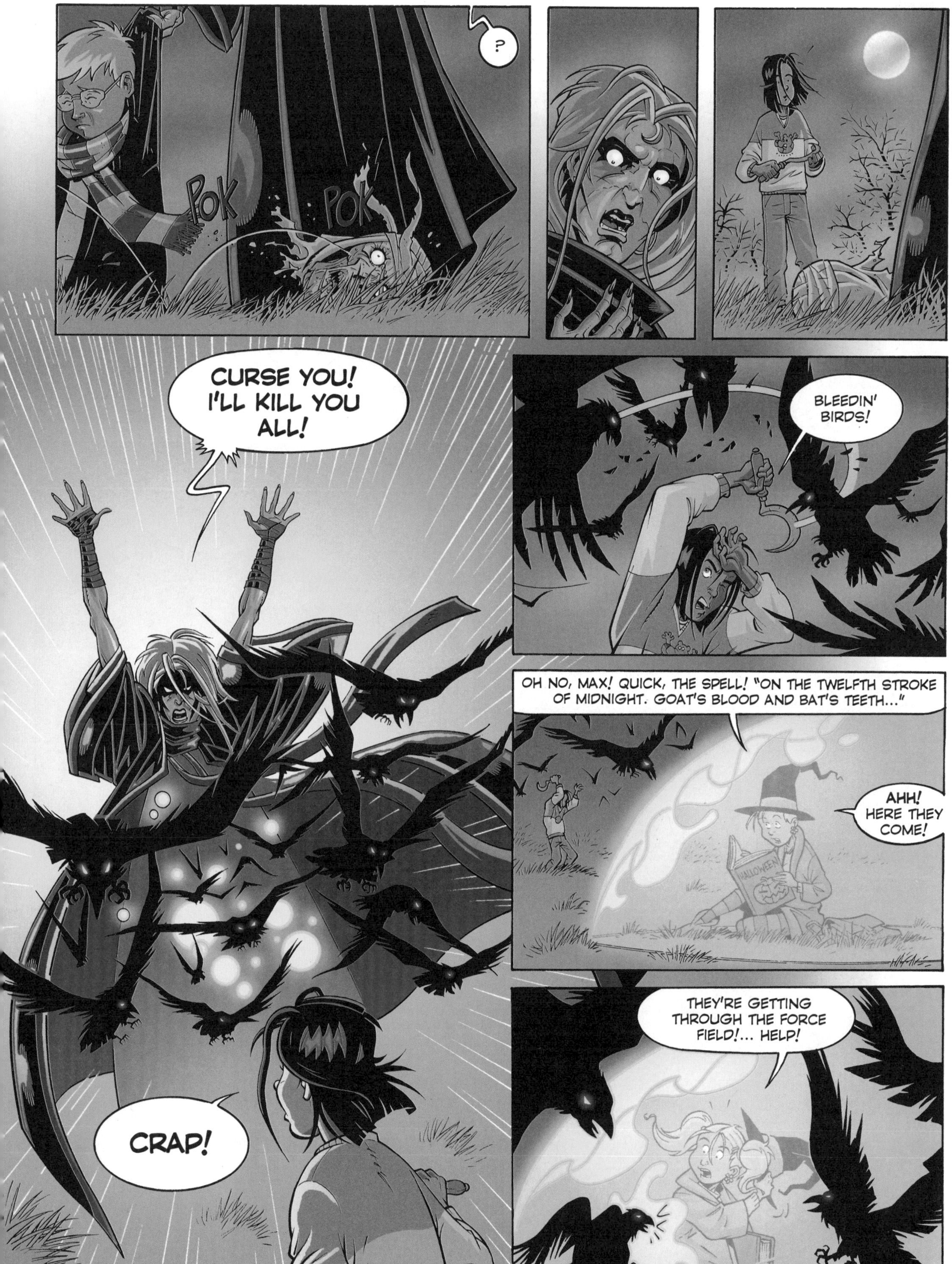
POK
POK
?
CURSE YOU! I'LL KILL YOU ALL!
BLEEDIN' BIRDS!
OH NO, MAX! QUICK, THE SPELL! "ON THE TWELFTH STROKE OF MIDNIGHT. GOAT'S BLOOD AND BAT'S TEETH..."
AHH! HERE THEY COME!
HALLOWEEN
CRAP!
THEY'RE GETTING THROUGH THE FORCE FIELD!... HELP!
39

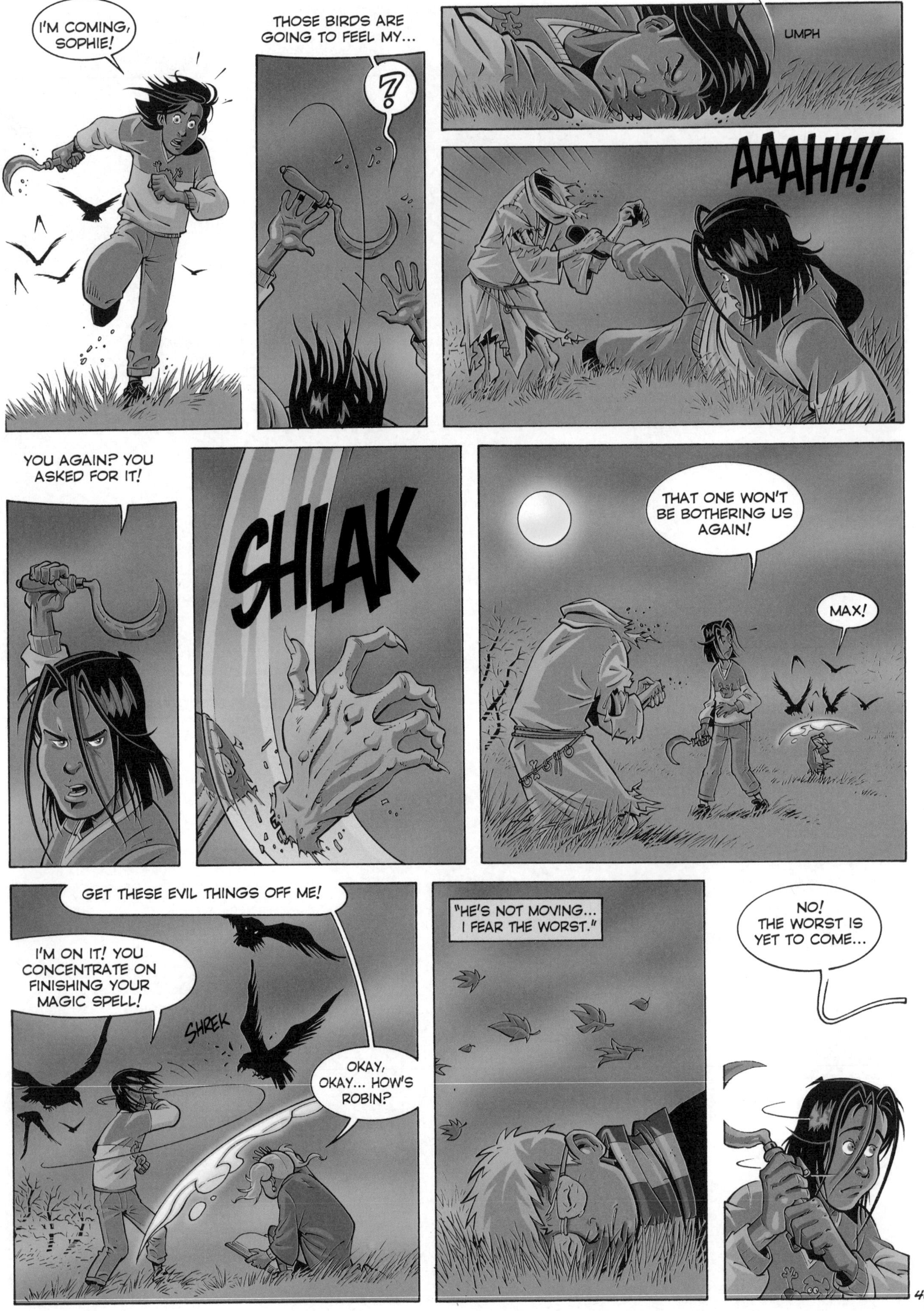
I'M COMING, SOPHIE!
THOSE BIRDS ARE GOING TO FEEL MY...
?
UMPH
AAAHH!
YOU AGAIN? YOU ASKED FOR IT!
SHLAK
THAT ONE WON'T BE BOTHERING US AGAIN!
MAX!
GET THESE EVIL THINGS OFF ME!
I'M ON IT! YOU CONCENTRATE ON FINISHING YOUR MAGIC SPELL!
SHREK
OKAY, OKAY... HOW'S ROBIN?
"HE'S NOT MOVING... I FEAR THE WORST."
NO! THE WORST IS YET TO COME...
40

YOU'RE GOING TO REGRET COMING UP AGAINST US... IT'S TIME TO END THIS GAME!

YOU'RE RIGHT, EMMA... LET'S FINISH IT!

WHERE WAS I? "DEVIL'S DAUGHTERS, TREMBLE ON YOUR BROOMS: SPIT OF TOAD, HAIR OF FERRET, RANCID MUSHROOMS..."

I'LL TRY TO HOLD THEM BACK FOR AS LONG AS POSSIBLE... YOU SEND THEM BACK TO WHERE THEY CAME FROM AS QUICK AS YOU CAN!

"IT'S TOO LATE NOW, WITCHES IN HATS ..."

YAAAH!

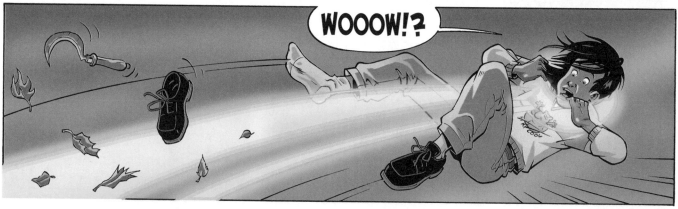

WOOOW!?

CRAP! COUGH! COUGH! ARE YOU NEARLY DONE? COUGH!

YES, YES! STOP INTERRUPTING ME, WILL YOU?! "BEAK OF CROW AND EYE OF DEAD RAT..."

"LEAVES OF OAK AND LOCK OF WHITE HAIR. EVIL SORCERERS, DISAPPEAR INTO THIN AIR!"

THERE! I'M DONE...

BUH?

41

THE COMET! IT'S GONE... GOODBYE, SISTER.

BOP

WOW... IT WORKED! I MANAGED TO DESTROY TWO WITCHES WITH A CHILDREN'S BOOK!

TSHHH TSHHH

MAX, DID YOU SEE? WE GOT THEM! WELL, CORRECTION... I GOT THEM. 'CAUSE IF I HAD TO COUNT ON THE TWO BOYS LOOKING AFTER ME...

YOU'RE THE BEST! LOOK... THERE ARE ONLY ASHES LEFT...

LET'S GO AND SEE ROBIN.

SO, MATE? IS THAT THE ONLY WAY YOU FOUND TO AVOID FIGHTING?...

BRO, ARE YOU OK? YOU THINK YOU'LL BE ALL RIGHT?

W... WHAT A HALLOWEEN NIGHT.

YOU HAVE TO ADMIT IT WAS MORE ORIGINAL THAN ASKING FOR SWEETS.

TRUE!... I DON'T REGRET COMING OUT WITH YOU GUYS!

"HEY! I RECOGNIZE THIS PATH... WHAT?!... THE WITCHES' HOUSE ISN'T THERE ANYMORE..."

"NO, SOPHIE. IT MUST HAVE DISAPPEARED WITH THEM... LIKE ALL THEIR SPELLS. WELL, I HOPE."

"DID THOMAS BECOME HUMAN AGAIN, THEN?"

"SIS... THOMAS IS DEAD."

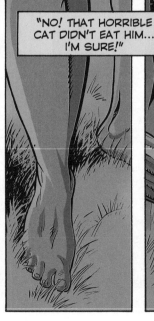

"NO! THAT HORRIBLE CAT DIDN'T EAT HIM... I'M SURE!"

WHAT ON EARTH AM I DOING HERE, ALL NAKED?...

42

THE NEXT DAY

ARE YOU SURE YOU DON'T WANT TO TRY MY PALM TREE ALCOHOL?

BLAM

I BROUGHT IT BACK FROM ONE OF MY MANY TRIPS TO AFRICA...

THERE! TAKE THAT!

AND THAT, TOO!

THANKS, BUT I'LL STICK TO THE PORT.

BLAM
BLAM
BLAM

BLAM

SUCH VIOLENCE! SOMETIMES MY OWN SON SCARES ME...

BLAM

OH, YOU SHOULD SEE IT AS A HEALTHY RELEASE, NOTHING TO WORRY ABOUT...

WHAT'S THE GAME, THEN?

YOU HAVE TO KILL AS MANY WITCHES AS POSSIBLE!

CAT, DON'T YOU DARE!

AND BELIEVE ME, MUM. WE'RE THE BEST AT THAT GAME!

DINNER!

AH!

YES!

WHERE'S SOPHIE?... ROBIN, CAN YOU CALL YOUR SISTER?

SOPHIE!... DINNER!

43

SOPHIE, IT'S READY! WHAT ARE YOU DOING?

I'M COMING!

CLICK

FWOOS

44

ASTAROTH...

HAHAHAHA

THE END

SEPTEMBER 2002

46

1 – THE VAMPIRE FROM THE MARSHES

2 – MALEVOLENCE AND MANDRAKE

COMING SOON

3 – IN THE SHADOW OF THE BEAST

SEE YOU SOON